woods

Meadow

Meet Your New Friends,
Lulu and Max

LULU

Lulu is spunky, smart, and smacks her bubble gum with great enthusiasm. In her backyard is a wooded area with lots of trees. But to Lulu it is the grandest forest in all the land with talking animals and plenty of adventures waiting for her and her friend Max!

MAX

Max is always with Lulu! They are best friends. He has superpowers— or at least he thinks he does. He wears glasses that make him feel like he can run faster, jump higher, and see farther. Even though Max also loves to explore the forest, he is very responsible and makes sure all the details are taken care of as Lulu dreams up all kinds of adventures.

A gift for: ....

From: ....

Win or Lose, I Love You

© 2015 by Lysa TerKeurst, LLC

Published in Nashville, Tennessee, by Tommy Nelson. Tommy Nelson is an imprint of Thomas Nelson. Thomas Nelson is a registered trademark of HarperCollins Christian Publishing, Inc.

Illustrated by Jana Christy

Interior design by Christina Quintero

Tommy Nelson titles may be purchased in bulk for educational, business, fund-raising, or sales promotional use. For information, please e-mail *SpecialMarkets@ThomasNelson.com*.

Library of Congress Cataloging-in-Publication Data is on file.

ISBN-13: 978-0-5291-0400-7

Mfr: DSC/Shenzhen, China/September 2015/PO# 9350149

Printed in China

15 16 17 18 19 DSC 6 5 4 3 2 1

Lulu
and her Tutu

Win or Lose

I Love You!

LYSA TERKEURST

Illustrated by JANA CHRISTY

Tommy NELSON

A Division of Thomas Nelson Publishers

NASHVILLE   MEXICO CITY   RIO DE JANEIRO

Hi friend,

As a mom who has walked five kids through everything from soccer games to school elections, I can honestly say that one of the greatest lessons a parent can teach his or her child is how to navigate life's wins and losses. But it's also one of the most difficult lessons to teach.

Here's the thing—sometimes kids struggle with bad attitudes, wanting to get ahead, and constantly wanting to put themselves first. Winning and losing can become all-consuming to the point where our children can really forget that God has a plan in all of this—whether they win or lose.

Recently, my daughter Brooke ran for office at her school. I watched her work so hard, spending endless hours on campaign materials and talking points. She really wanted this! As I helped her navigate the election, I recognized that this was much more than an opportunity for her to run for a position. It was an opportunity for me to come alongside her and teach some really impactful life lessons.

So when she didn't win, we talked through the truly important things: finishing well, keeping a good attitude, and embracing the fact that her value wasn't determined by this event.

Please know that I'm praying for you and your kids as you read through this book. I'm praying that these lessons live in their hearts as they march past the days of playground games and school elections to become the God-following adults they're meant to be.

I've also written out a list of Scripture memory verses that will be helpful to tuck into your kids' hearts or stick on their mirrors, to equip them with the most powerful tool—God's Word!

Many Blessings,

"Come on, Max. Hurry!"
Lulu called as she pulled the heavy wagon.
"Do you own anything we *aren't* carrying to the
forest today, Lulu?" Max asked.

"Today is the Field Day competition to choose the leader of the forest," Lulu explained. "We have so many fun games for the animals to play, and we get to be the judges! But," she warned with a serious look on her face, "we might have to help them. The winners will be doing happy dances. But the losers might be sad . . . and maybe even a little mad."

At the Tall, Tall Tree, just past the Very Merry Berry Bushes, Lulu and Max found an itty-bitty bear and a great big chipmunk, a masked rabbit and a long-eared raccoon, a furry goose and a feathered coyote.

"Lulu," Max whispered. "The animals are all mixed up!"

"That means it's time for the Costume Contest!" Lulu giggled.

Lulu and Max took a careful look at each costume before making a decision.

"Coyote wins with his clever wings!"

Lulu finally announced.

"I won! I won!" Coyote yelled. "I'm the best!"

"Waahhhhh!"

Goosey wailed. "*I* have the best wings! *My* wings are real." Goosey sat on a stump and cried while the other animals tried to cheer her up.

"Uh-oh," Max whispered. "You were right. Goosey's being a poor loser . . . and Coyote's being a poor winner."

Lulu jumped into action.

"Now everyone, remember: you may not win, but you must try. Sometimes you'll lose, but there's no need to cry. Win or lose, one thing that's true . . . no matter what, I love you!"

Just then, Bear-Bear rushed up, nodding his head. "Congratulations!" he told Coyote. Then he turned to Goosey. "Your beautiful wings inspired Coyote to make his costume! Isn't that super?"

Lulu gave every animal a beautiful stick she had decorated.

"It's time for the stick toss," she announced.

"I love my stick, Lulu!" Bear–Bear said. "I want to keep it forever!"
"Thanks, Bear–Bear!" Lulu grinned.
"One . . .

two . . .

three . . .

throw!"

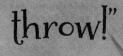

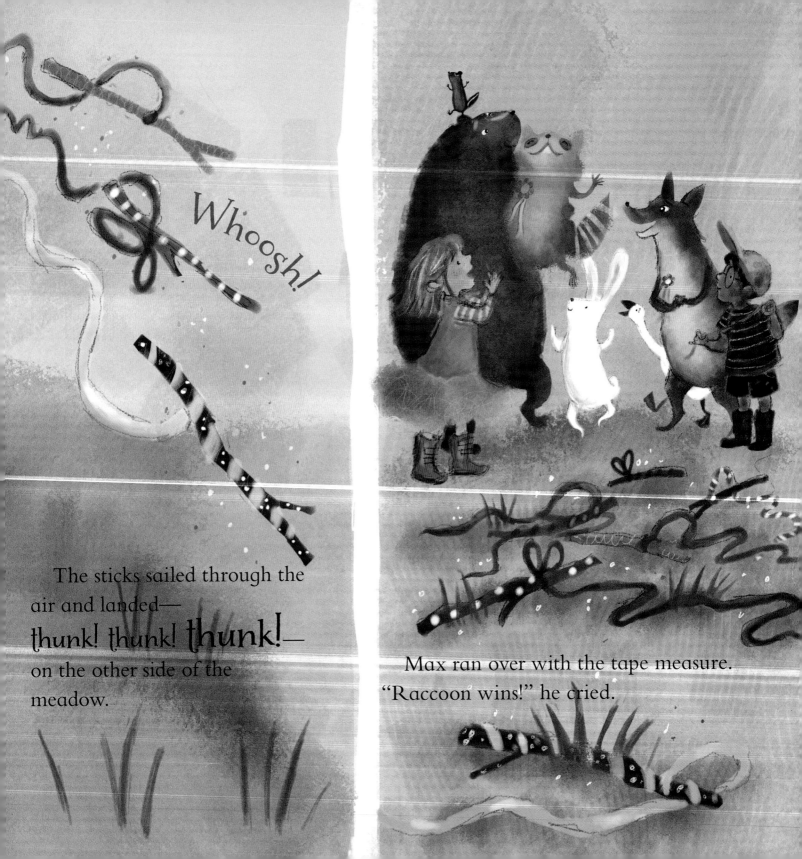

Whoosh!

The sticks sailed through the air and landed—
thunk! thunk! thunk!—
on the other side of the meadow.

Max ran over with the tape measure.
"Raccoon wins!" he cried.

"Time to set up the obstacle course," Lulu
announced. "Raccoon, since you won the stick toss,
would you please pick up the sticks?"

"Do I have to?" Raccoon whined.

"Don't worry—I'll help," Bear-Bear told him.

"Now I understand why we brought all this stuff," Max said as he and Lulu went to work. "But when do we get to eat those pies?"

"The last event is a pie-tasting contest," Lulu said. "I can't wait to try Bear-Bear's pie. He's the best baker in the forest!"

BALL KICK!

When the obstacle course was ready,
the animals lined up.
"I'm definitely going to win!" Coyote bragged.
"I'm the fastest animal in the forest—"

"On your mark," Lulu called.

"*And* I've been practicing for *weeks*," Coyote boasted.

"Get set," said Max.

"There's nobody faster than—" Coyote continued.

"Go!" Max and Lulu yelled together.

Zoom! All the animals raced off, leaving Coyote behind!

"Wait! No fair!" Coyote cried. "I wasn't ready!"

"Go, Coyote! Hurry!" Lulu urged him.

Coyote scrambled to catch up. He passed Bear-Bear at the Hula Hoop Loop, Chipmunk at the Tinsel Tunnel, and Rabbit at the Raised Rock. Only Goosey was still ahead of him. Coyote pushed forward with all his might . . . but it was too late. Goosey crossed the finish line and won the race!

"Goosey wins! Hooray!" Lulu cheered.

"NOOOOOOOOOOOOOOOO!"
Coyote howled. "I WANTED TO WIN!"
He stomped over to the pie table and
kicked it as hard as he could.

Crash!

Crunch!

Smash!

The pies splattered all over the meadow,
turning it into a sticky, icky mess! Worst of all,
there wasn't a single Very Merry Berry pie left
for the pie-tasting contest.

"Oh, Coyote," Lulu said sadly. "What have
you done?"

Coyote hung his head. No one knew what to say—until Bear-Bear stepped forward. "We can clean this mess!" he announced. "We'll get some water and soap—"

"I have sponges in my burrow," Rabbit chimed in.

"That's just what we need!" Bear-Bear said. Soon clouds of bubbles filled the air as everyone worked together. All the animals were laughing and having fun . . .

except one.

Lulu found Coyote in the clearing
by himself.

"It's okay to lose, you know," Lulu began. "Sometimes you'll lose. Other times you'll win. What matters most is how you treat your friends."

"I ruined Field Day," Coyote said miserably. "I'm the worst animal in the forest."

Lulu hugged him. "Coyote, you behaved badly, but *you* aren't bad. What can you do to make things better?"

Coyote knew just what he needed to do.

Coyote took a deep breath and walked over
to the animals. "I'm sorry for taking the fun
out of Field Day," he said. "I wanted to win so
badly that I forgot how to be a good sport . . .
and a good friend."

"I was a poor sport too," Goosey said.
"I'm sorry."

"Bear-Bear," Coyote said, "You were so excited about the pie-tasting contest. I'm sorry I ruined it."

Bear-Bear smiled. "I forgive you, Coyote. We don't have any pies left . . . but we can still have a picnic!"

As the animals munched on the Very Merry Berries Lulu brought, Rabbit asked, "Who will be the **leader** of the forest? Coyote, Raccoon, and Goosey tied."

"I guess the judges will have to choose," Chipmunk said.

"A leader's job is to make things better," Lulu said. "Even though others won contests, Bear-Bear made Field Day better for everyone. He worked hard all day long. He was kind and encouraging, friendly to everyone . . ."

"And **forgiving**," Coyote added.

Lulu and Max bent their heads together and spoke so quietly that no one could hear them. At last, it was time for the big announcement.

"Bear–Bear, we think *you* should be the leader of the forest!"

"Me?" Bear-Bear gasped in amazement.

When all the animals cheered, it was clear they agreed.

"Thanks, everybody,"
Bear-Bear said.

"A lot of responsibility comes
with winning—and with losing—
and especially with being a leader.
I promise I'll always do my best.
Who wants to watch the sunset
from the Tall, Tall Tree?"
"We do!" everyone cried.

As the animals climbed the Tall, Tall Tree, they turned Lulu's lesson into a song and sang together:

"You may not win, but you must try.
Sometimes you'll lose, but there's no need to cry.
Win or lose, one thing that's true—
No matter what, I love you!"

10 Biblical Words of Wisdom Whether You Win or Lose

1. Work willingly at whatever you do, as though you were working for the Lord rather than for people. COLOSSIANS 3:23 NLT

2. "Do to others as you would have them do to you." LUKE 6:31 NIV

3. Don't rejoice when your enemies fall; don't be happy when they stumble. PROVERBS 24:17 NLT

4. Love one another with brotherly affection. Outdo one another in showing honor. ROMANS 12:10 ESV

5. Therefore, if anyone is in Christ, the new creation has come: The old has gone, the new is here! 2 CORINTHIANS 5:17 NIV

6. Above all, love each other deeply, because love covers over a multitude of sins. 1 PETER 4:8 NIV

7. Don't push your way to the front; don't sweet-talk your way to the top. Put yourself aside, and help others get ahead. Don't be obsessed with getting your own advantage. Forget yourselves long enough to lend a helping hand. PHILIPPIANS 2:3–4 THE MESSAGE

8. God opposes the proud but gives grace to the humble. JAMES 4:6 NLT

9. But he said to me, "My grace is sufficient for you, for my power is made perfect in weakness." Therefore I will boast all the more gladly about my weaknesses, so that Christ's power may rest on me. 2 CORINTHIANS 12:9 NIV

10. Let us not become weary in doing good, for at the proper time we will reap a harvest if we do not give up. GALATIANS 6:9 NIV

mountains   Tall, Tall Tree

Forest

Very Merry
Berry
Bushes